Dedicated to my mother, Georgina, without whom
this book wouldn't exist. Also to my father, Stephen, my sister,
Louisa, and my husband, Tom, for their endless support.

BIG PICTURE PRESS

This edition published in the UK in 2022 by Big Picture Press.
First published in the UK in 2020 by Big Picture Press
an imprint of Bonnier Books UK
4th Floor, Victoria House
Bloomsbury Square, London WC1B 4DA
Owned by Bonnier Books
Sveavägen 56, Stockholm, Sweden
www.bonnierbooks.co.uk

1 3 5 7 9 10 8 6 4 2

ISBN 978-1-80078-128-3

This book was typeset in Cabrito Didone
The illustrations were created with watercolour,
pencil and ink and finished digitally

Edited by Carly Blake
Designed by Olivia Cook & Marty Cleary
Production by Neil Randles

Printed in China

MIX
Paper from
responsible sources
FSC® C020056
FSC
www.fsc.org

Sarah Maycock

Sometimes
I feel...

B P P

Sometimes

I feel as

BIG

as a

Bear.

But there will always
be someone bigger
than me and sometimes
I will feel small.

Sometimes

I feel as

HAPPY

as a

Lark.

But not all days can be filled with song . . .

. . . and sometimes I will need time
before I can join in with the chorus.

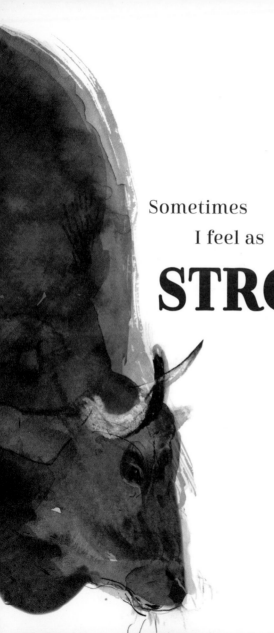

Sometimes
I feel as

STRONG

as an
Ox.

But the days that leave me
worn out and weary
will make me stronger tomorrow.

Sometimes

I feel as

B U S Y

as a

Bee.

But slowing down to see the beauty all around me is time just as well spent.

Sometimes
I feel as

BRAVE

as a
Lion.

But when the roar of the storm
seems frightening . . .

. . . I know it will pass
and so will my fear.

Sometimes

I feel as

CUNNING

as a

Fox.

But when I'm too clever
for my own good,
I get caught out.

Sometimes
I feel as

HUNGRY

as a
Horse.

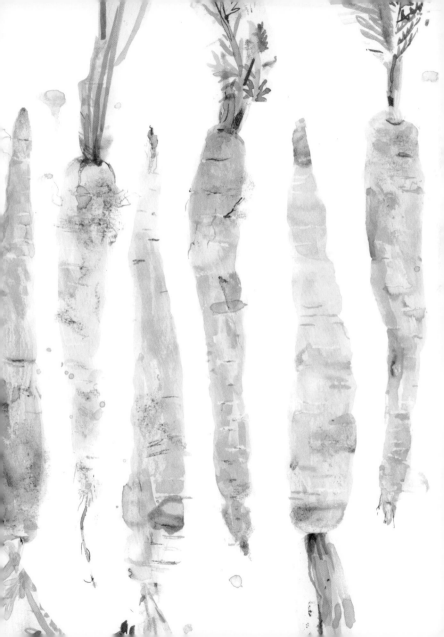

But stopping when
I've had enough . . .

. . . means there's plenty left
for everyone else.

Sometimes

I feel as

CuRiOuS

as a

Cat.

But it's impossible to know
the answers to everything . . .

. . . and sometimes
I have to give my
mind a rest.

Sometimes
I feel as

BLIND

as a

Bat.

But when the way
ahead is unclear . . .

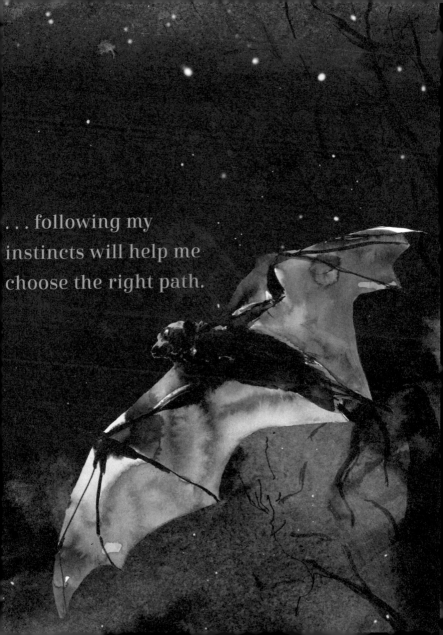

. . . following my instincts will help me choose the right path.

Sometimes

I feel as

TIMID

as a

Mouse.

But if I stand tall, I can
find my inner courage . . .

. . . and come
to feel . . .

. . . as
BIG
as a
Bear.

A note from the artist

This book began its life in 2011 as my final year project at Kingston University. I wanted to explore the universal nature of animals and how we can relate them to our own experiences and characteristics. In each animal I painted, I saw a feeling that at face value seemed simple, but was there was another side? In looking closer, there is empathy, and in relating, there is self-awareness.

Animals provide an endless way to explore my favourite media, ink and watercolour. I spent time drawing at London Zoo and working from nature documentaries to really see how they move and love thinking about how swooping brush marks could capture a living form. I will never tire of drawing animals.

Sarah Maycock